# Mop Top

# Crabtree Publishing Company
www.crabtreebooks.com

PMB16A, 350 Fifth Avenue
Suite 3308,
New York, NY

616 Welland Avenue
St. Catharines, ON
L2M 5V6

Published by Crabtree Publishing in 2008

First published in 2006 by
Franklin Watts
(A division of Hachette Children's Books)
338 Euston Road
London   NW1 3BH

Text © Sue Graves 2006
Illustration © Maddy McClellan 2006

The rights of the author and the illustrator of this Work
have been asserted.

Cataloging-in-Publication data is available at the Library of Congress.

ISBN 978-0-7787-3857-2 (rlb)
ISBN 978-0-7787-3888-6 (pbk)

**Series Editor:** Jackie Hamley
**Series Advisor:** Dr Hilary Minns
**Series Designer:** Peter Scoulding

Printed in the U.S.A.

# Mop Top

by Sue Graves

## Illustrated by Maddy McClellan

**Crabtree Publishing Company**

www.crabtreebooks.com

**Sue Graves**

"I don't have a dog, but I do have a cat. Luckily, I don't have to worry about keeping the hair out of her eyes, unlike poor Henry with Mop Top."

**Maddy McClellan**

"I had a dog called Skipper when I was Henry's age. I got him for my birthday and I was SO excited that I ignored all my friends!"

Henry's puppy had
a shaggy coat.

He was so shaggy
that everyone called
him Mop Top!

But Mop Top's coat
grew …

... and grew!

Mom tied it up
into bunches.

11

# But that was no good.

13

Dad gave Mop Top
his hat.

15

# But that was no good.

17

Then Henry had an
idea. He told Mom.

They went to
see Annie.

Annie gave Mop Top
a haircut.

21

"Now Mop Top has a crop top!" laughed Henry.

# Notes for adults

**TADPOLES** are structured to provide support for early readers. The stories may also be used by adults for sharing with young children.

Starting to read alone can be daunting. **TADPOLES** help by providing visual support and repeating high frequency words and phrases. These books will both develop confidence and encourage reading and rereading for pleasure.

**If you are reading this book with a child, here are a few suggestions:**

1. Make reading fun! Choose a time to read when you and the child are relaxed and have time to share the story.

2. Talk about the story before you start reading. Look at the cover and the blurb. What might the story be about? Why might the child like it?

3. Encourage the child to reread the story, and to retell the story in their own words, using the illustrations to remind them what has happened.

4. Discuss the story and see if the child can relate it to their own experiences, or perhaps compare it to another story they know.

5. Give praise! Children learn best in a positive environment.

## If you enjoyed this book, why not try another TADPOLES story?

**At the End of the Garden**
9780778738503 RLB
9780778738817 PB

**Bad Luck, Lucy!**
9780778738510 RLB
9780778738824 PB

**Ben and the Big Balloon**
9780778738602 RLB
9780778738916 PB

**Crabby Gabby**
9780778738527 RLB
9780778738831 PB

**Five Teddy Bears**
9780778738534 RLB
9780778738848 PB

**I'm Taller Than You!**
9780778738541 RLB
9780778738855 PB

**Leo's New Pet**
9780778738558 RLB
9780778738862 PB

**Little Troll**
9780778738565 RLB
9780778738879 PB

**Mop Top**
9780778738572 RLB
9780778738886 PB

**My Auntie Susan**
9780778738589 RLB
9780778738893 PB

**My Big, New Bed**
9780778738596 RLB
9780778738909 PB

**Pirate Pete**
9780778738619 RLB
9780778738923 PB

**Runny Honey**
9780778738626 RLB
9780778738930 PB

**Sammy's Secret**
9780778738633 RLB
9780778738947 PB

**Sam's Sunflower**
9780778738640 RLB
9780778738954 PB